This edition published by Parragon in 2011

Parragon
Queen Street House
4 Queen Street
Bath BA1 1HE, UK

Aladdin

PaRragon

Bath • New York • Singapore • Hong Kong • Cologne • Delhi
Melbourne • Amsterdam • Johannesburg • Auckland • Shenzhen

In the vast Arabian desert, an evil sorcerer named Jafar told a thief named Gazeem to enter the Cave of Wonders to fetch a magic lamp.

As Gazeem walked toward the cave, which was in the shape of a tiger's head, a voice boomed:

"Only one may enter here, one whose worth is far within—the Diamond in the Rough!" The thief continued, and slowly stepped into the tiger's mouth—but its jaws slammed shut!

"What are we going to do now?" Iago, Jafar's parrot, asked.

"I must find this . . . Diamond in the Rough," Jafar declared.

The next evening in the city of Agrabah, a poor young man named Aladdin and his monkey, Abu, sat down to eat their first meal in days.

But Aladdin realized that there were others worse off than he, and he gave the bread to some hungry children. The two friends went home with empty bellies.

"Someday, Abu, things are going to change," Aladdin said as he stared out at the Sultan's palace. "We'll be rich . . . and never have any problems at all."

Meanwhile, in the palace, Princess Jasmine was very unhappy. Her father, the Sultan, wanted her to marry a snooty prince—in three days' time!

"It's the law," he had told Jasmine. "You're a princess."

"Then maybe I don't want to be a princess anymore," she had replied as she patted her tiger, Rajah. "If I do marry, I want it to be for love."

"I've never even been outside the palace walls," Jasmine said sadly to herself.

The Sultan was at his wits end! He called upon his most trusted advisor for help—the grand vizier, Jafar.

"Jafar, I am in desperate need of your wisdom," the Sultan pleaded. "Jasmine refuses to choose a husband."

"Perhaps I can devise a solution," Jafar said. "But it would require the use of the mystic blue diamond."

The Sultan did not want to give up his cherished ring. But Jafar used his snake staff to hypnotize him, then took the ring!

By the time the sun set, Jasmine had decided to run away. "I can't stay here and have my life lived for me," she told Rajah. "I'll miss you." Then she climbed over the palace wall.

On the other side, Jasmine suddenly found herself alone in a new world—Agrabah's bustling marketplace.

The beautiful princess quickly caught the attention of Aladdin, and he began to watch her.

Seeing a hungry child, Jasmine plucked an apple from a fruit stand and gave it to him.

"You'd better be able to pay for that!" bellowed the huge fruit seller. The princess hadn't realized she would have to pay. Luckily, clever Aladdin stepped in and helped her get away.

"So, where are you from?" Aladdin asked, leading Jasmine to his rooftop home.

"I ran away," Jasmine answered with a sigh. "My father is forcing me to get married."

"That's awful," Aladdin agreed.

11

Back at the palace, Jafar had used the Sultan's ring to find out who was the one who could enter the Cave of Wonders. An image of Aladdin had appeared! Jafar quickly ordered the Sultan's guards to find the young man and bring him to the palace. Jasmine had tried to save him by revealing she was the princess, but the guards didn't listen.

Locked away in a dungeon, Aladdin could think only of the beautiful princess he would never see again. Luckily, Abu showed up and unchained him.

Suddenly, an old prisoner stepped out from the shadows. "There is a cave filled with treasure," he whispered. "Treasure enough to impress your princess."

Aladdin was intrigued by the story and followed the old prisoner through a secret passage and into the desert. Soon, he and Abu were standing before the Cave of Wonders! The tiger let Aladdin pass—but instructed him not to touch any of the treasure, only the lamp.

"Fetch me the lamp, and you shall have your reward," the old man promised.

Through the mouth of the cave, Aladdin and Abu followed the steep steps down, down, down . . .

They met a friendly Magic Carpet who happily led them to the magical, golden lamp resting on an altar.

Just as Aladdin reached for the lamp, his greedy monkey grabbed a sparkling gem! The voice of the cave spoke:

"You have touched the forbidden treasure! You shall never see the light of day again!"

They reached the entrance. But as soon as the old man had the lamp, he drew a dagger out of his sleeve and Aladdin dropped into the collapsing cave. Abu bit the man, but he was thrown down after Aladdin.

"It's mine!" the man shrieked, pulling off his disguise to reveal that he was Jafar! As he reached into his robe for the lamp, he realized it was gone!

"Nooo!" he cried.

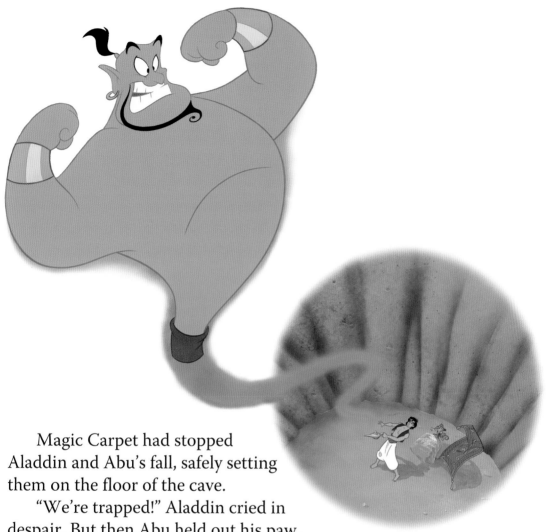

Magic Carpet had stopped Aladdin and Abu's fall, safely setting them on the floor of the cave.

"We're trapped!" Aladdin cried in despair. But then Abu held out his paw.

"The lamp!" Aladdin exclaimed. The monkey had snatched it back.

Aladdin looked at the lamp. "I think there's something written here, but it's hard to make out." He rubbed the lamp to clean some of the dust off. The lamp began to glow. Then a towering cloud of smoke poured from the spout—and took the form of a giant blue genie!

"Say, you're a lot smaller than my last master," the genie said, looking down at Aladdin.

Aladdin couldn't believe that he had his very own genie! "You're going to grant me any three wishes I want?"

Aladdin didn't want to waste a wish, so he tricked the Genie into transporting them out of the cave. "How about that!" the Genie bragged as they all soared over the desert on the Magic Carpet.

"What is it you want most?" the Genie asked, offering Aladdin the first of his three wishes.

"Can you make me a prince?" Aladdin asked. He wanted to impress Princess Jasmine.

"Hang on to your turban, kid!" the Genie shouted. "We're gonna make you a star!"

Meanwhile, Jafar was desperate to become Sultan. But without the magic lamp to help him, he had to come up with a new plan.

Whoever married Princess Jasmine would be the new Sultan, so the villain used his snake staff to hypnotize the Sultan.

"You will order the princess to marry me!" Jafar commanded.

Dressed from head to toe in royal robes, Aladdin went to the palace to speak to Jasmine's father. "Your Majesty, I have journeyed from afar to seek your daughter's hand in marriage," Aladdin announced. The Sultan was thrilled! But Jasmine thought Aladdin was just another snooty prince.

To win Jasmine's heart, Aladdin sneaked up to her balcony on his Magic Carpet. "Princess Jasmine, please give me a chance," Aladdin pleaded. Then he invited her on a moonlight ride.

Jasmine realized that this prince was really the young man she had met in the marketplace. By the end of the night, they had fallen in love!

Jafar heard that Aladdin, disguised as Prince Ali, and Jasmine were growing close. Jafar knew he had to get rid of the prince.

He ordered his guards to chain Princes Ali up—and throw him into the sea!

Luckily, the Genie was nearby and Aladdin used his second wish to save himself.

"Don't scare me like that, kid," the Genie said as he unchained his master.

Aladdin raced to the palace on his Magic Carpet—just as the hypnotized Sultan was about to order Jasmine to marry Jafar!

"Your Highness, Jafar has been controlling you with this!" Aladdin cried as he smashed the snake staff.

"Traitor!" the Sultan cried. But before the guards could arrest Jafar, the villain escaped.

Later, hiding in his laboratory, Jafar plotted.

"Prince Ali is nothing more than Aladdin!" he said. "He has the lamp!"

At dawn the next morning, Iago crept into Aladdin's room and stole the lamp.

At last Jafar had the lamp! Eagerly, he rubbed it, and the
Genie appeared.

"I am your master now!" Jafar bellowed. "I wish to rule . . .
as Sultan!"

The Genie was powerless to resist.

"Genie, no!" Aladdin screamed as Jafar took over the palace.
"Sorry, kid," the Genie said. "I've got a new master now."
Then Jafar made his second wish—to become a powerful sorcerer!
Jafar used his evil sorcery to banish Aladdin to the snowy ends of the earth! Luckily, Abu and the Magic Carpet were still with him.
"Now, back to Agrabah!" Aladdin cried as they sped off on the Magic Carpet.

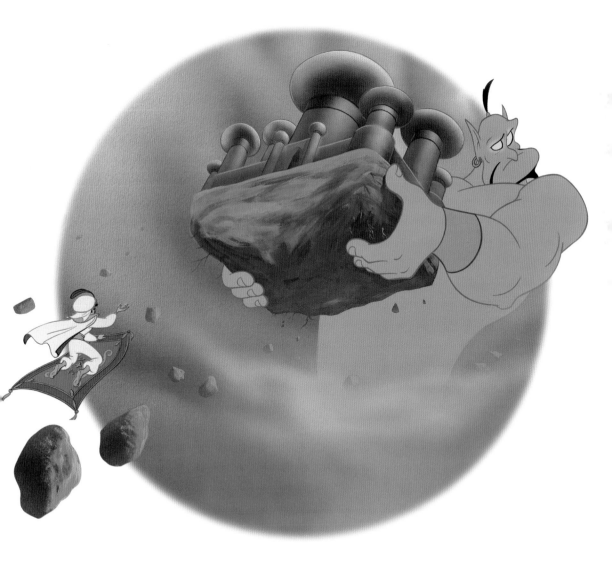

Back at the palace, the poor Sultan was hanging from the ceiling of his throne room like a marionette. And Jasmine was Jafar's slave!

Jafar was so busy enjoying his power, he didn't notice Aladdin sneaking into the throne room. Just as Aladdin reached for the magic lamp, Jafar saw his reflection in Jasmine's tiara.

"How many times do I have to kill you, boy!" the villain shrieked as he fired his snake staff at Aladdin and trapped him.

Jasmine ran to help her hero.

"Princess, your time is up!" Jafar said, trapping Jasmine in a huge hourglass.

"You cowardly snake!" Aladdin shouted.

"Snake, am I?" Jafar hissed. The villain turned himself into a gigantic cobra!

Suddenly, Aladdin had an idea that he thought might rid the city of evil Jafar for good.

"The Genie has more power than you'll ever have!" Aladdin taunted Jafar.

So the power-hungry Jafar used his last wish to become a genie.

But the villain forgot one important detail—all genies must live within a lamp until they are summoned by a new master.

"Noooo!" Jafar cried as he was imprisoned inside a magic lamp—forever!

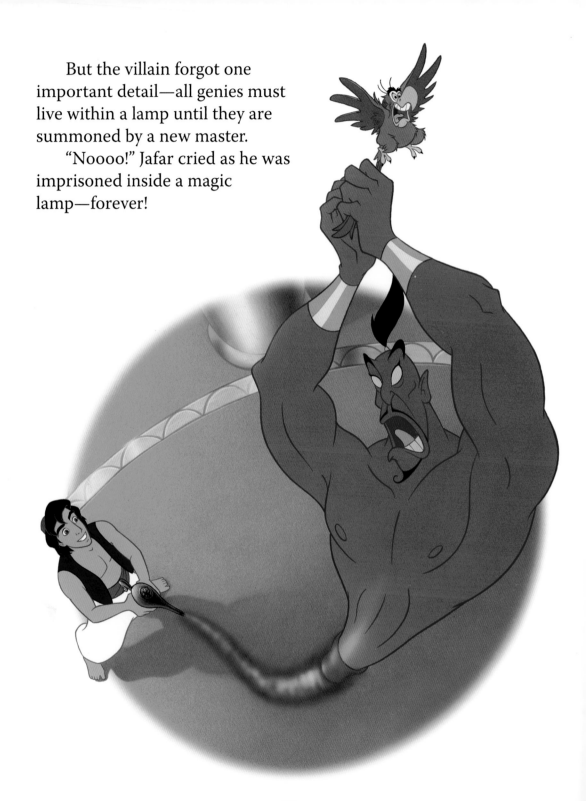

Aladdin used his third and final wish to set the Genie free. And the Sultan changed the law so that Princess Jasmine could marry anyone she chose.

"I choose you, Aladdin," Jasmine said as she kissed her prince. And they all lived happily ever after.

The End